MR. LITTLE go to the Festival

Roger Hargreaves

Original concept by
Roger Hargreaves

Written and illustrated by
Adam Hargreaves

> Hello, my name is Walter. Can you spot me in this book?

When the envelope landed on Little Miss Giggles' doormat, she giggled with excitement. It was the tickets she had bought for the Happyland Festival.

Two tickets.

One for herself and one for her best friend, Little Miss Shy.

Little Miss Shy was not quite as excited as Little Miss Giggles.

Little Miss Shy didn't like crowds. But she really wanted to go.

And with Little Miss Giggles' encouragement, they packed up the car and drove to the festival.

Little Miss Shy was feeling so shy when they arrived that she put up their tent in a matter of moments and retreated into it.

Little Miss Giggles wanted to go and explore the festival, but she could not coax poor Little Miss Shy out of the tent!

Little Miss Giggles got quite a surprise when she did leave.

Mr Muddle had pitched his tent next door.

However, his tent was the wrong way up!

Little Miss Giggles giggled to herself, what a muddle he was!

And there was much more to make her giggle.

She wandered down to the main field where all the food and activities were.

She giggled at all the people dressed in costumes and outlandish hats.

And she giggled at Mr Silly, who was playing his bubble-blowing trumpet.

What a crazy, fun place the festival was!

Then Little Miss Giggles discovered a face painting tent.

She came out as a tiger.

And this gave her an idea.

She persuaded the face painter to come back to her tent where she explained her idea to Little Miss Shy.

Who came out as a leopard!

"There!" cried Little Miss Giggles. "You're in disguise. Nobody will know who you are, so there's no need to feel shy!"

And it worked.

The two of them had lots of fun at Little Miss Fun's Funfair.

They giggled at the stilt walkers.

And were amazed by the fire breather.

But then it rained.

It didn't stop Little Miss Giggles giggling. Nothing could dampen her spirits!

But it did start to wash off their face paint.

"Oh no!" cried Little Miss Shy, who rushed back to their tent.

In no time at all, the crowds had churned the festival site into a sea of mud.

Mr Messy loved the mud.

But Little Miss Splendid did not.

And neither did Mr Small!

"Help!" he cried.

Little Miss Giggles had to come to his rescue.

It turned out that Mr Small's tent was nearby, but it was so tiny that it had been washed away by the rain, so Little Miss Giggles invited Mr Small to stay in their tent.

That night, after the rain had stopped, they all sat round a campfire and toasted marshmallows.

Little Miss Shy was still too shy to leave the tent, but she did manage to toast her marshmallow!

The next morning, Little Miss Shy got up very early to go to the toilet, but there was already a long queue when she got there.

Little Miss Shy looked at the queue.

How could she stand in this queue with everyone knowing why she was queuing?

She blushed at the very thought of it.

And decided she could wait.

When the bands started playing, Little Miss Giggles wanted to set off early to be at the front of the audience.

But poor Little Miss Shy could not bring herself to leave the tent.

So, Little Miss Giggles went with Mr Small.

But in the crowd Mr Small could not see anything.

Suddenly a pair of hands lifted him up in the air.

It was Mr Tall.

And a Mr Tall bird's-eye view of the stage!

Little Miss Giggles loved the music, but it wasn't the same without Little Miss Shy. She missed her friend and wanted her to enjoy it too.

And then she had another idea.

She rushed back to the tent and explained her idea to Little Miss Shy.

And it worked.

The crowd watching the band were all facing the stage and no one noticed Little Miss Shy at the back of the audience. She and Little Miss Giggles danced all day and all night long!

Little Miss Shy had never enjoyed herself so much. It was the perfect end to the festival.

The next day, Little Miss Giggles dropped Little Miss Shy off at her home.

Little Miss Shy said a quick goodbye and sprinted upstairs to the bathroom.

A toilet without a queue!

Bliss.

And a bath.

Double bliss!

And then Little Miss Shy caught sight of herself in the mirror.

She was covered in mud and paint … what a sight!

But what fun!